Albert,

I Want to Show You Something

Deborah Colliander

ISBN 978-1-63630-035-1 (Paperback)
ISBN 978-1-63630-036-8 (Digital)

Covenant Books, Inc.
11661 Hwy 707
Murrells Inlet, SC 29576
www.covenantbooks.com

To my grandchildren Magdalene, Gavin, Anna, and Alex: I want to show you something.

It was a sunny day at the ocean-side. Albert awoke early, excited to get to the shoreline and find some fresh clams. Landing in the sand, Albert's foot touched something sticky. Picking up one foot, Albert noticed something stuck on it. Trying to shake this sticky mess free, Albert realized shaking was not going to work.

"Maybe if I ask my friends to help me I can get this sticky mess off."

"Harry, Gabe, I sure can use some help over here!"

Wondering what the problem is, Harry and Gabe walked down the shore.

"Hey Albert, how can we help you?"

"I stepped in something really sticky and I can't get it off my foot!"

"Can you pick your foot up?" asked Gabe.

Picking up his foot, Gabe could see that Albert had stepped on gum.

"Albert, you have gum stuck on your foot!"

"Well, how do you think I can get this gum off of my foot?"

Harry was thinking maybe he could pick it off with his beak.

"Albert, let me try to pick it off for you!"

Albert agreed that this might work.

"Ouch," said Albert as he put his foot back down in the sand.

"Oh, I'm sorry, I guess I picked a little too hard!"

Hearing the still small voice, "Albert, I see you are in a bit of a mess."

"I sure am. I stepped into something that I now wish I hadn't."

"Albert, do you know that you aren't the first one to step in a sticky mess?"

"Well, I sure feel sorry for anyone that does. I am really stuck!"

"Albert, did you see that sticky gum before you stepped on it?"

"No, or I wouldn't have stepped on it!"

"Well, do you know that many times in our lives problems will arise that seem to come out of nowhere. One doesn't see them coming! And they can be pretty sticky messes too!"

"I do remember one day I was caught in a big wind storm. I was really enjoying the day soaring inland when suddenly I was being carried out over the sea. I couldn't control my wings."

"I'm sure you were rather frightened!"

"I was more than frightened. I thought I would never survive!"

"Albert, do you know that when you are trusting Jesus you will find some good in every circumstance, even if it seems very dark at the time? When strong winds come and they seem to be directing one off course, this may be the right direction in one's life. Many times in life, one seems to be stuck and have a feeling of going nowhere. Old ways of doing things are not working. This is when one needs to take a step and walk into the new."

Finding a rock, Albert started scraping the gum off of his foot. It seemed to be coming off easier than when Gabe was pecking at it.

Thinking of many of his friends living ordinary lives, Albert couldn't wait to find them.

Leaving the sticky gum behind, Albert motioned to Harry and Gabe to come with him. Noticing Gabe was preoccupied near another rock, Albert questioned this delay.

"Gabe, what's up?"

"Well, it seems I found where you had stepped before!"

While scraping the gum off his foot, Gabe exclaims, "I'm finding this new way is better than the old way!"

Harry, waiting patiently for Albert and Gabe, shouts, "Let's go, guys, I'm not sticking around here any longer with you!"

Laughing, they all left together to share the new.

2

"Skippity doo dah, skippity ay, my oh my, what a wonderful day!"

Skipping along the beach one sunny morning, Albert loved jumping into the puddles along the shoreline. Noticing others walking along the beach, Albert was attracted to their feet. He saw many different kinds and colors of shoes on their feet.

Looking at his own feet, Albert wondered if he could ever have a pair of shoes to walk in and began imagining what it might feel like to put his foot in a shoe.

Walking further along the beach, Albert spotted a pair of yellow flip flops sitting in the sand.

"Oh I wonder if I could just try them on!"

Albert walked up to the flip flops and felt it was alright to try them on as no one was around them. Albert balanced on one foot and stuck his right foot into the flip flop.

"This does feel a little strange," said Albert.

Sticking his left foot in the other flip flop, Albert felt as though he had two new feet. Picking up his right foot, Albert took one baby step forward. Then picking up his left foot he took another step. Taking a few more steps, Albert realized he was really walking in shoes...someone else's shoes!

"I love these shoes!"

Albert began to walk a little faster. He began to notice that people were beginning to gather around where he was walking. He could see them smiling. Some were actually laughing out loud. Children began to gather and delight in what they were seeing.

Albert's friend Harry was flying overhead and noticed Albert and all the people who had gathered near him. Harry saw that Albert had something on his feet and began to question him.

"Albert, what do you have on your feet?"

"Shoes, I have shoes on my feet! Follow me Harry and watch me walk."

Walking a little faster down the shore, Albert found it to be somewhat harder walking in these shoes.

"Hey, Albert," called a little child watching. "I wish I could fly like you!"

The child began to chase him. Albert began to walk even faster. Realizing he was being chased, Albert decided it was time to fly. He took a few steps to fly and found he couldn't leave the ground.

"Oh my, have I forgotten how to fly?"

Albert tried again but just couldn't lift off.

Hearing the still small voice, "Albert, I see you are having a hard time trying to fly."

"Yes, and this had never happened before."

"Albert, what do you have on your feet?"

"I have shoes I found on the beach. I wanted to see what it would be like to walk in shoes."

"Do you know whom these shoes belong to?"

"No, but I sure like walking in these shoes."

"Hey, Albert, I wish I could fly like you," the little child shouted again as she was just standing and watching Albert trying to fly.

Hearing the still small voice, "Albert, I see you are still having trouble flying."

"Yes, I just can't get the lift off I need."

"Albert, I know you like walking in these shoes but you are not meant to wear shoes. These shoes are holding you back. You were created to fly just the way you are."

Stepping out of these shoes, Albert took a few steps and had the perfect lift off that he needed to fly.

The little child watched as Albert soared high above her.

Walking over to the shoes Albert had left behind, the little child stepped into them. They were a perfect fit.

Now walking back down the beach the little child wondered if she was really flying.

3

Feeling rather joyful one day, Albert began to sing.

> Sometimes I wonder and sometimes I see,
> Not knowing where I'm going but feeling
>   so free.
> I have such joy springing up from within,
> It makes me laugh, it makes me grin.
> I see my friends just wondering too,
> I wonder if they feel just as I do!

"Albert, do you know why you are feeling so happy?"

Albert loved hearing from his newfound friend, the Holy Spirit.

"I'm not sure but I do love this feeling right now."

"Albert, do you like to discover new places that you have never been to before?"

"Oh yes I do, I love the new!"

"Albert, follow me, I want to show you something."

Leaving the ocean-side and soaring higher, Albert notices green grass and white fences below. He also notices a big red barn.

"Albert, soar lower now, I want you to see something new!"

Landing on a white fence post, Albert notices an animal he had never seen before. Wondering just what this animal is, he begins to hear a whinny sound.

"Oh my, what is this?"

"Albert, this is a horse. I have created many other animals as well in my kingdom on earth. They are all your friends too. Would you like to meet some new friends?"

"Oh yes I would!"

"Okay, let's go inside this barn."

Entering through two big red doors, Albert hears all kinds of new sounds. He hears many baas and cluck clucks and hee haws and even familiar sounds of birds. Hearing a mooing sound, Albert decided he would be safer up on a high rafter.

"Everyone is very different in here!"

"Yes, Albert, I created them this way. Do you know that each animal has a special purpose in life just as you do?"

"What are their purposes?"

"The mooing sound you heard came from a cow. The cow provides milk. The baaing sounds are from sheep and goats. They provide meat and milk as well. The chickens who make the sounds of cluck clucks provide meat and eggs. The hee haw sound you heard is from the donkey. Do you know that many years ago the donkey was used in a very special way?"

"No, but I would like to know how."

"When Jesus was sent to earth many years ago, he came as a baby. His father Joseph and his mother Mary were traveling to the town of Bethlehem to pay their taxes. At this time, Jesus was about to be born. Mary rode for many miles on the back of a donkey traveling from Nazareth to Bethlehem. When they arrived in Bethlehem they could not find a room to stay. They went to an inn that was also full but the kind innkeeper offered them room in a stable. In this stable, Jesus was born in a manger."

"You mean Jesus was born in a place where animals stayed and his bed was where the animals ate out of?"

"Yes, Albert, he was. Jesus was born for a mighty purpose here on earth. He was the son of God, given to us as a gift. From the life of a baby to a grown man, Jesus taught us how to live in his kingdom here on earth. Jesus gave his life on the cross so that in our hearts today Jesus can live."

"Albert, do you know that you were created for a mighty purpose?"

"Well, I would like to think I am but I'm not sure what it is."

"Albert, before we came to this barn I heard you singing the happiest song about being free. You are free to be happy and joyful because Jesus who lives in your heart has set you free. He is your joy. In the song you were singing I heard that you were wondering if your friends were feeling this way too. Do you know that your life makes a difference in your friends' lives? When they see you happy and joyful, I am sure that they would like to be happy and joyful too."

"Oh that would make me even happier if my friends were feeling this way!"

Leaving the high rafter and flying out of the big red barn doors, Albert knew he had to find his friends. Landing on the shore, Albert notices a group of his friends. Wandering closer, Albert calls to his friends.

"Hey guys, follow me, I have something to show you."

Flying to the big red barn, Albert and his friends enter through the two big red barn doors. His friends were delighting in meeting Albert's new animal friends. Then Albert directed them to the manger where the animals were feeding.

"Do you know that you were born for a purpose?"

4

"Albert, Albert, wake up!"

"What did you say?"

"I said wake up! It's a beautiful day and you are still sound asleep. Do you know it is almost noon?"

"Oh my, I must have been tired!"

"Yes, you must have. Why are you so tired?"

"Well, probably because I have been working so hard."

"What have you been working at?'

"You know how I experience all these wonderful truths and it makes me so happy I just have to go and tell my friends?"

"Albert, that is why I created you."

"But when I try to tell my friends sometimes they just don't seem to want to listen."

"Albert, do you know how I just woke you up?"

"Yes, I was pretty sound asleep."

"Well, do you know that your friends are sound asleep? They may look awake, but inside they are sound asleep. They see what they want to see. They hear what they want to hear and they say what they want to say. Albert, I am here to help you. You don't have to work so hard. Just ask me to help. I love waking up people! Watch!"

Mabel and Ina were talking together at the shoreline. They seemed to be talking about Gloria.

"Ina, did you just question me?"

"No, why?"

"Well, I just heard someone telling me to be careful what I hear!"

"No, I was just telling you about Gloria."

"Oh, I kind of feel like I don't want to hear about Gloria now. I'll be back later."

Standing alone, Ina began to feel uneasy inside. Hearing the still small voice, Ina questions, "What did you say?"

"I said be careful what you say."

Thinking about Gloria and her problems, Ina knew they didn't belong to her and Mabel. Ina left the shoreline looking for Mabel. Over on a rock Ina found Mabel and Albert talking.

Wide awake now and without hesitation, Albert full of joy calls to Ina. "Ina, come join us!"

Hearing that still small voice once again, "Albert, remember, just ask, just ask!"

5

"Let's go sailing," called Albert to his friends.

"What is sailing?" they asked.

"It's when you look for the fishing boats and find all the fresh fish."

Following Albert, his friends soared out over the sea. Not too far out, Albert spots a fishing vessel. He could already smell the sweet scent of fish.

"Come on, guys, fly lower now and follow that boat!"

Soaring lower they can now see the fishermen pulling in nets full of fresh fish.

"Do you know that these fishermen are our friends? "Watch this!"

Flying lower, Albert snatched a small fish from the fisherman's hand. Delighting in this gift, Albert nodded his head in thankfulness. The fisherman motioned to the other seagulls that they had scraps to give to them as well. Soon all of Albert's friends joined in with this feast.

Resting on the high mast of the vessel, Albert was delighting in watching his friends being fed.

"Albert, I want to show you something."

Hearing the still small voice, Albert began to listen.

"I want to tell you a story from long ago. One day there were fishermen who were fishing all day and night.

But they didn't catch anything. One of the fishermen was Simon Peter. Jesus had instructed Peter to row his boat out in the deep waters and to cast his nets and that he would catch many fish. Peter reminded Jesus that they had been fishing all day and night and hadn't caught anything. Peter and the fishermen rowed out into the deeper waters and let down their nets. When they pulled up their nets they were amazed to see such a huge catch of fish. All of their nets were about to burst! Albert, when you leave everything behind to follow Jesus, you will have it all. Jesus will be your everything."

Understanding what he heard, Albert began to realize many of his friends reminded him of these fish.

"I know my friends must be hungry to know about Jesus too."

Seeing his friends still feasting on the fish from the fishing boat, Albert calls to them to follow him. Excited to share with his friends, Albert told them the story of Peter and his miracle catch of fish.

"Come on guys, I need to show you something more about fishing!"

Soaring together Albert and his friends left everything behind and followed the still small voice. They knew there was more that they were called to do. A new mission of fishing was ahead for them.

"Don't worry guys, you won't even have to clean the fish, Jesus does!"

6

"Albert, I love hearing you sing."

"I love to sing more these days. The songs I sing make me smile. I will sing songs that I have never heard before. They just kind of show up from inside of me. This morning when I awoke and flew to the shore, I was singing the words, *wonderful words of life.* I kept singing these words over and over. Oh how I wished my friends would sing more too."

"Albert, I want to show you something. Start singing these words again over here by this big rock."

Albert went over to the big rock and started to sing. While singing even new words kept coming to Albert. He began to notice that he wasn't singing alone on this rock. Many of his friends began gathering around him. This made Albert want to sing even more.

"Albert, what are you singing?" asked Bertha, one of his new friends.

"Just keep listening and you will hear what I am singing."

Albert began to sing about wonderful words of life. When he was singing, he felt as though he wasn't even there. New words and sounds began to bubble up right out of him. He had never laughed and sang at the same time.

Watching in amazement, his friends that began to gather also began to dance back and forth to this beautiful music.

"Albert, may we sing along with you?" asked Charlie, one of Albert's new friends.

"Oh yes, Charlie, please join me in singing!"

Charlie began to sing. He felt as though he wasn't there too. Bertha began to sing. Mabel began to sing. Ina began to sing. Many others joined in and the sounds of heaven were flowing out of all of them.

Harry and Gabe began to laugh as they were singing.

"We can hardly sing any more," laughing harder and harder.

Tears began to flow from Albert's eyes.

"Oh my, what am I feeling?"

Hearing the still small voice, "Albert, I have just shown you what can happen when my life in you touches my life in your friends. You are experiencing the wonderful words of life I have given to you. In these words of life there is love, and joy, and peace, and healing. Albert, I have anointed you for my purpose. This anointing on you touches your friends' lives and sets them free from hardships that they live. My life in you is my power going forth to set the captives free and to show them how to live in my kingdom here on earth."

Watching his friends still dancing and singing, Albert felt as though he was already in heaven. A new song began to arise in Albert.

Heaven touching earth, I feel the fire,
Thank you, Holy Spirit, that you have
  taken me higher.
Flying higher in this heavenly place,
I know it's your love and supernatural grace.

Bertha, still singing and laughing, decided to stroll down the shoreline from the group. Soaring above Bertha, her friend Alice noticed her singing and laughing.

"Bertha, what are you doing? You sure look and sound happy!"

"Come down and I will show you."

Landing, Alice caught on very fast, singing and laughing as well. Soon another group of friends were following them.

Albert heard the still small voice again, "It's pretty amazing to see your friends flowing in my spirit isn't it?"

Hopping down from the big rock, Albert seemed to be walking a little crooked.

"Oh my, I seem to be a little wobbly."

Laughing, the Holy Spirit spoke, "Albert, you are just fine. You have just tasted my new wine."

Still walking rather unsteady, Albert began to sing.

I have just had a taste of this new wine,
Oh yes it is truly of the divine.
Bubbling up from my belly within,
Seems I'm walking with a big new grin.
Oh come dear friends taste and see if you
  would,
Just follow me, I want to show you
  something good!

7

"Albert, Albert, what's up?"

Soaring lower and noticing Harry was waving to Albert, he began to laugh. Albert couldn't stop laughing. He laughed so hard he had to find a place to rest.

"Albert, what's so funny?"

Albert couldn't even begin to talk as he was still laughing.

"Albert, what is so funny? Are you laughing at me?"

"Oh no, Harry, I am feeling such joy within myself that I can't even express why I am laughing!"

"How can you laugh when you don't even know what you are laughing at?"

Hearing the still small voice, Albert began to listen.

"Albert, tell Harry that when you are laughing it is not you laughing."

"Really? How will Harry understand that when I don't even understand it?"

"Albert, how do you feel when you are laughing?"

"I feel such joy that I can't even express this feeling. I feel love, and peace, and joy unspeakable. I can hardly get the words out!"

"Do you know why you can't get the words out?"

"Why?"

"Because they are my words. My words are always full of love, and peace, and joy unspeakable. My words express who I am in you. When my spirit ignites your spirit an exchange takes place. All of me is manifested through you. Joy is one of the gifts of the spirit. My gift is touching your heart and spirit and this is when my joy comes forth through you. Do you know that sometimes others will catch my joy through you?"

After this short rest and listening, Albert started to talk with Harry and tell him why he was laughing. Trying to get the words out, he noticed Harry was beginning to laugh.

"Oh my," said Harry. "I feel such joy. I feel like I am flying and I am standing here in this sand!"

Laughing with Harry, Albert didn't have to explain this new found joy. Harry understood.

8

"Albert."

"Oh hi, friend, I've been wondering where you have been."

"I noticed you were looking rather sad. Is there something that is troubling you?"

"Well, not anything that I can really think of, but I do feel rather sad. How come some days I feel so happy and free and then other days I feel so sad and hopeless?"

"Albert, I want to show you something."

"First of all, I am so happy that we have become friends and that you listen and follow me now. I love how much higher you are flying. I'm sure you love the new warmth of the winds at this new height."

"Oh yes I do! When I am soaring in this high place, I am free, and happy, and find that even fear is gone."

"Albert, I want to ask you a question. I noticed you staring out at the ocean. Have you ever wondered why the ocean waters come in and go out at different times of the day?"

"Well, I know there are better fishing times and better finds along the shore when the waters come and go."

"Albert, do you see the waves in the water?"

"Oh yes, I love floating on them and looking for fish."

"These long period waves are caused by a gravitational pull of the moon and sun. This is what is called a tide. When the tide comes in to shore it is called a flood current. The outgoing tide is called an ebb current. In these long period waves there will always be a high tide and a low tide. I'm sure you'll find a lot of good clams when the tide comes in!"

"Oh yes, and I have figured out how to crack these hard shells!

Listening to his newfound friend, Albert is beginning to sense that there is something very important he wants to show him through these tides.

"When I noticed you looking rather sad I knew I needed to explain a few things to you. Albert, you have God's life and spirit in you. You also have a soul. This is where your feelings reside. Also your will, and emotions, and intellect reside in your soul. When God first created you, he breathed the breath of life into you which became your spirit. When your spirit came in contact with your body, your soul was produced. Albert, do you know that you commune with me in your spirit? This is where I dwell, in the secret place of the most high. When you look out into the ocean you see many waves. Some days they are small and some days they are big. The waves always end up on the shore. We are like waves moving with the tides.

In our lives there can be many different types of waves. We can have waves of joy and waves of peace and also waves of sadness. We can have waves of hope as well. But the greatest wave is the wave of faith. This wave of faith will always carry us safely to shore. Jesus is faith and he always rides the waves with us. Even when the strong winds come and fear may arise in our soul, Jesus is there to calm the winds. Albert, the tides always come in and go out. It is that way with one's life. Here on earth, some days we may feel happy and some days we may feel sad. But always remember, within a given day and night, you are never alone.

There are seasons in our life's journey. Remember that riding the waves with Jesus, no matter if you are at high tide or low tide, he is always there to meet you on the shore."

Looking out into the ocean, Albert could hardly wait to catch that big wave. He knew the tide was turning and his friends needed to catch this wave too.

9

Sitting alone on a cement wall by the ocean, Albert is feeling quite alone. Lately he has been noticing that there is a difference at the ocean-side. On an ordinary day there are many scraps of food left behind. Also Albert had been noticing so few people enjoying the beaches. Albert senses in his spirit that everyday living is not the same as it was, a tear falls from his eye.

"Albert, I want to show you something."

Hearing the still small voice, Albert begins to not feel so alone.

"Albert, I see you sitting all alone on this beautiful day. I know you are feeling sad. If you listen to me now I want to show you something. I am aware of what is happening by the ocean-side here. It is not only here but all across this world. Albert, you are seeing and feeling exactly what everyone else is experiencing. In your sadness, I see you sensing aloneness, confusion, fear, and even death. You see, Albert, in this world that you live in, there is good and evil. When this world was first created it was designed to be all good. Sad to say, the evil one came in and there has been destruction ever since. The evil one comes to kill and destroy and cause great harm in the lives of people. A plague has crippled this world when this evil moved into

many countries. Albert, I want to show you how you can overcome your many feelings. Remember me telling you about Jesus?"

"Oh yes, I love hearing about Jesus."

"Jesus is your everyday friend too, Albert. You belong to him. He walks with you every day."

"Do you know why you love hearing about Jesus?"

"Why?"

"Because you feel his love touching your heart. Jesus's one word to all of us is to love one another. When one loves another, all fear is gone. There isn't any fear when love takes its place. There are many people in this world today that need to know Jesus and his love. Do you know that when you gather with your friends that Jesus is there too? You may not see him but you will always feel his presence and his love."

At this very moment Albert began to feel so loved his fear was gone.

"I must find my friends. I must show them there is a greater way to overcome this turmoil in our midst!"

Soaring higher and looking below for his friends, Albert sees them. Albert notices that they are all near a flagpole at the beach. Landing near the flagpole, Albert walks over to his friends. Immediately he could see they were looking rather forlorn and anxious. Asking the Holy Spirit to give him words to say to his friends, words of love arose in his spirit.

"Hi, friends, today is the most beautiful day in the world!"

Looking up at Albert, Gabe questions Albert.

"Albert, how can you say today is the most beautiful day in this world? Haven't you seen what is going on?"

"Oh yes, but I have something to show all of you."

Asking the Holy Spirit again for the perfect words to tell his friends, Albert hears the still small voice.

"Albert, you have already shared with your friends about me and my love. Now ask your friends why they love me."

Even questioning himself, Albert knew this was going to be the best answer to all this turmoil.

"Hey, fellas, I have a question I need to ask you. Why do you love Jesus?"

Thinking and talking among themselves there was a moment of silence.

"Albert, tell them this answer they need to hear. Because I first loved you!"

Suddenly it looked as though a bright light showed around them all.

Looking up at the flag, all Albert could say was "Oh glory!"

10

Flying to the top of the flagpole, Albert could see from a new height. Not only seeing from a distance but seeing something new in his spirit, he knew that his heart had been touched in a special way.

Albert kept thinking about the light that showed all around him and his friends. Within this light there was a new feeling of joy and peace. A feeling he never experienced before. He had to know more.

Hearing the still small voice, "Albert, I see that you are at rest on top of this flagpole."

"Yes, I am resting here but not really at rest. Could you please explain to me what just happened with me and my friends and what was that bright light?"

"Albert, what you were experiencing is my glory."

"But what is glory?"

"Glory is my presence. When Jesus was here on earth, he lived in the heavenly realm. Glory is the atmosphere of heaven. Albert, this is your day!"

"What do you mean this is my day?"

"Albert, when you woke up this morning you were already in my day that I had given to you. I was there to meet you. Albert, do you hear the birds singing when you wake up at dawn?"

"Oh yes, when I wake up at dawn I love to sing!"

"Albert, this is my song in you. You are singing out of this special glory realm. Your songs are praises unto me. I love it when you first wake up and I can greet you!"

"Albert, when you sing songs of joy, these are heavenly praise songs. This is a time of worship. When one is worshiping me, my glory comes forth and shines all around. Within my glory you are full of my joy and renewed strength. You are a carrier of my glory."

"My light and glory will always dispel the darkness. The world was in darkness when I created this world. I spoke four words and my light and glory was created here on earth."

"What were those words?"

I said, "Let there be light!"

Albert became very quiet remembering a very dark night flying over the ocean back to his home. Thinking about the fear he felt, he began to tremble inside.

"Albert, what's wrong?"

Trembling in his thoughts, Albert began to speak.

"I remember one very dark night flying home. I flew over the ocean and it was very hard to see. The waves were tossing high and the wind was very strong. I had never felt so very alone, helpless, and lost. Suddenly there was another seagull flying right next to me. I began to cry as I felt such peace, comfort, and stillness come over me. We both flew home safely."

"Albert, if I told you that was me flying with you, would you believe me?"

A tear fell from Albert's eye.

"Oh Holy Spirit, I am beginning to know who you really are! I must go and find my friends. I need to show them something."

Albert flew off of the flagpole and headed to shore. As the tide was coming in, Albert saw his friends searching for new clams.

"Hey, fellas, I need to show you something!"

"We have been looking for you, Albert, where have you been?"

"I was on top of the flagpole feeling rather restless but my restlessness has turned into something glorious!"

"There's that word again, Harry!" Gabe exclaimed.

"What word, Gabe? asked Harry.

"Glory. I heard Albert use it at the flagpole."

"Yes, fellas, this is just what I want to show you!'

Albert began hearing the still small voice, "Albert just show them who I am."

"Oh glory, this is going to take a while! Okay, fellas, let's go over to that puddle by the shore."

Gathering all around the puddle, Albert asked his friends to look into the puddle. In great wonderment, Albert's friends stood amazed at their new reflections. Remembering the light that showed around them at the flagpole, they began to understand.

With waves of his glory washing over them leaving the shore, Albert and his friends began to soar with their new wings. Catching the wind of his spirit, they were on their way, being carried into greater things!

"This is who I am"

About the Author

Deborah Colliander, a wife, mother of two, and grandmother of four resides in Hampton Falls, New Hampshire. Walking with Jesus since Deborah's childhood, her inspiration comes from her special friend, the Holy Spirit. As an artist and writer, Deborah still creates from the child within.